DISNEY · PIXAR

Cars

TOON

HEAVY METAL MATER

& OTHER TALL TALES

Adapted by Frank Berrios

CONTENTS

Random House New York

Materials and characters from the movie *Cars*. Copyright © 2006, 2010 Disney/Pixar. Disney/Pixar elements © Disney/Pixar, not including underlying vehicles owned by third parties: Cadillac Coupe DeVille, Chevrolet Impala, and H-1 Hummer are trademarks of General Motors; Jeep® and the Jeep® grille design are registered trademarks of Chrysler LLC; Mazda Miata is a registered trademark of Mazda Motor Corporation; Mercury is a registered trademark of Ford Motor Company; Porsche is a trademark of Porsche; Volkswagen trademarks, design patents and copyrights are used with the approval of the owner, Volkswagen AG. Sarge's rank insignia design used with the approval of the U.S. Army. Background inspired by the Cadillac Ranch by Ant Farm (Lord, Michels and Marquez) © 1974. All rights reserved. Published in the United States by Random House Children's Books, a division of Random House, Inc., 1745 Broadway, New York, NY 10019, and in Canada by Random House of Canada Limited, Toronto, in conjunction with Disney Enterprises, Inc. Random House and the colophon are registered trademarks of Random House, Inc.

ISBN: 978-0-7364-2722-7

Library of Congress Control Number: 2010920459

www.randomhouse.com/kids

MANUFACTURED IN SINGAPORE

10 9 8 7 6 5 4 3 2

HEAVY METAL MATER

Lightning McQueen was enjoying the music at Flo's karaoke night. He turned to his friend Mater and asked, "Why don't you get up there and sing?"

"Nah, I don't want to steal the show," replied Mater as he started to tell Lightning McQueen a story. "I was a big rock star. . . ."

"I started out in a garage band," said Mater.
For a start-up band, they were pretty good.

In fact, Mater's band was so good, everyone wanted to know if they had a record. So the band decided to make one.

Everything was going pretty well at the studio—until a pesky fly got into the recording booth.

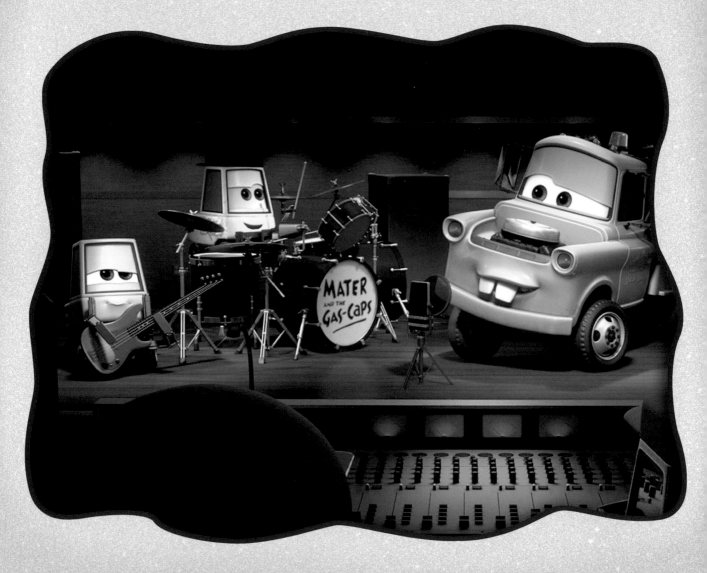

When the drummer tried to swat the fly with his drumsticks, he started to play faster and faster!

Mater had no choice but to sing faster and faster, too. He liked the new, heavier sound.

"Oh, yeah!" shouted Mater as he rocked on.

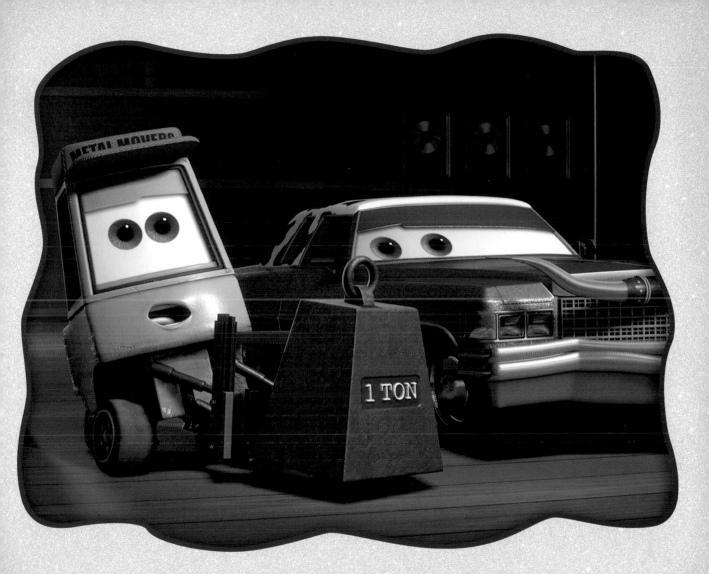

A music agent named Dex liked Mater's singing. "That sounds like angels printing money to me," Dex said. "All you need is a new name."

Mater thought for a moment. But before he could answer, a package arrived for him. "Where do you want this heavy metal, Mater?" asked the mover.

"That's it!" cried Mater.

And Heavy Metal Mater was born!

The band's shows sold out wherever they went.

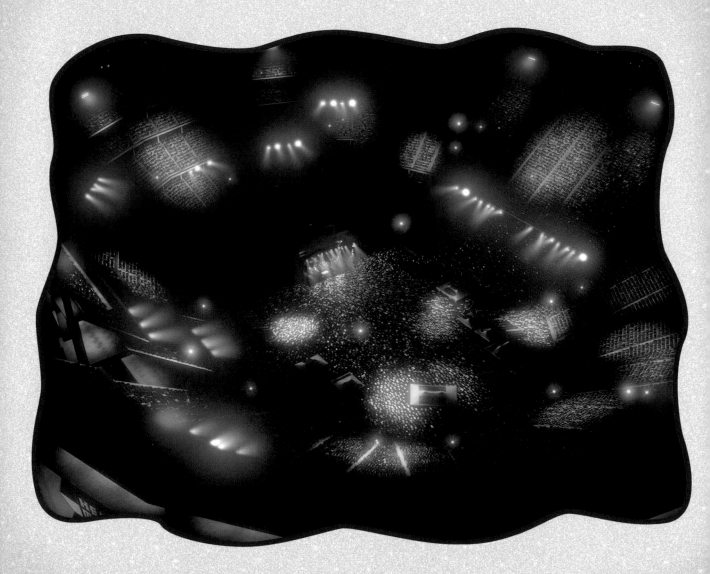

Heavy Metal Mater sported a cool new look that drove the band's fans wild.

Heavy Metal Mater really knew how to put on a show . . . lights flashed all over the stage, and the guitar solos were amazing!

Mia and Tia were super-fans. They never missed a show and knew the words to all of Heavy Metal Mater's songs!

Yep, Heavy Metal Mater was on top of the charts—and on top of the world. They were unstoppable!

The band closed every show with their most popular song, "Dad Gum." And just as they finished the tune, a giant Heavy Metal Mater balloon would rise from behind the stage and float over the audience as they screamed for more.

Lightning interrupted Mater's story.
"You were Heavy Metal Mater?" asked Lightning.
"No," replied Mater. "*We* was Heavy Metal Mater!"

"Are you ready to rock!" screamed Lightning as he jammed on the keyboard. He was in the band, too!

Lightning McQueen even joined Mater at the microphone for the big finale.

"I'm sorry, Mater. That did not happen," said Lightning McQueen.

"Well, suit yourself," replied Mater as he looked up into the sky.

UFM
UNIDENTIFIED FLYING MATER

Lightning McQueen and Mater were cruising down Main Street
when suddenly, a hubcap flew by.
    "Hey, look!" said Mater. "A UFO!"

"Mater, that was a hubcap," replied Lightning.

"No, it was a UFO," insisted Mater. "And I know 'cause I done seen one once."

"Yep, it was a crystal-clear night," Mater began, "when suddenly, a UFO popped up right in front of me!"

"Well, hey there. Welcome to Earth. My name is Mater."
"My name is Mator," replied the UFO.
"Should I take you to my leader?" asked Mater.
"Your leader," said the UFO.
"All right, then!" said Mater.

Mater took his new friend home with him.
"Well, here's all my liters!" announced Mater.

Mater was surprised at how thirsty the little UFO was.
"Buuurrpp!!" belched Mator after gulping down a huge barrel of oil.

"Yep, we did all my favorite things," Mater told Lightning McQueen.

"I taught him how to drive backwards," said Mater. "And he taught me how to fly."

Suddenly, helicopters swooped in and grabbed Mater's little buddy.
"Mator! I'll save ya!" yelled Mater.

Mater followed them to a secret base called Parking Area 51. He flew over a fence and quickly tried to find where they were holding the UFO.

When Mater saw his little friend surrounded by a group of scientists, he knew he had to act fast!

Mater snuck into the building and disguised himself as a doctor so he could get closer to the scientists surrounding Mator.

"Let's get outta here!" yelled Mater.

As Mater and Mator made a break for the exit, the scientists tried to stop them—but they failed!

Then tough-looking vehicles of every shape and size joined the chase!

"Whoa, whoa, whoa," said Lightning. "Do you really expect me to believe that you helped a UFO escape?"

"Well, you should," replied Mater. "You was there, too!"

"Aaaahhh!" screamed Lightning McQueen as he turned to see the military vehicles right on their tail!

Suddenly, all the cars slammed on their brakes.

"Whoa-ho!" said Mater as the Mother Ship appeared over the horizon.

"It's beautiful!" said Lightning just before he was beamed aboard
the Mother Ship, along with Mater and their little friend.

Then—*whoosh*—the giant Mother Ship blasted off into space.

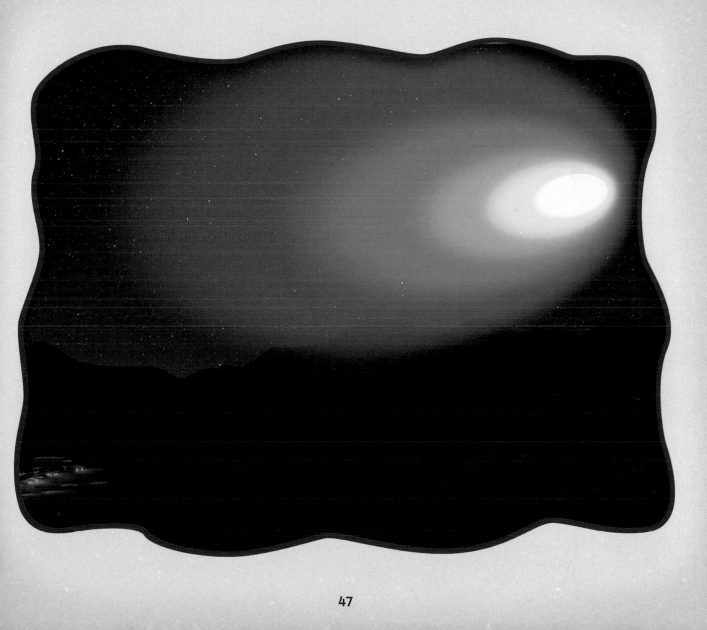

"Thanks for saving us, Mrs. UFO," said Mater. "You think you can drop us off at home?"

"Whoa!" screamed Lightning, falling from the Mother Ship.
"Thank you," said Mater as the ship flew off.

"I'm sorry, Mater," said Lightning, "that did not happen."

"Oh, yeah? Then how come I can do this?" replied Mater as he began to float away, thirsty for a liter after telling his story.

Tokyo Mater

Early one morning, Lightning McQueen and Mater were relaxing at Flo's. "Ya know, I used to be an import," Mater said.

"What? No way," said Lightning.

"Yes way," replied Mater. "It all started one day when I saw this car. . . ."

"Hey there, bud. Looks like you could use a tow somewhere," said Mater.
"Yes, but it is very far," replied the customer.
"Well, shoot," said Mater, "no tow is too far for Tow Mater."

"Man, I gotta change my slogan," said Mater as he drove out of the ocean and gasped for air. Mater had just towed the car halfway around the world—to Tokyo, Japan!

As Mater unhooked his customer, he accidentally bumped into Kabuto—the infamous drift racer!

Kabuto challenged him to a drift race to the top of Tokyo Tower.
To win the race, Mater would need some upgrades. Luckily, his two biggest fans, Mia and Tia, were in Tokyo, too!
"Modify!" yelled Mia and Tia.

Soon Mater had a new look—with modifications on everything from his tow cable and his tailfin to his wheels and his paint job.

He looked as if he could race. But could he really beat Kabuto to the top of Tokyo Tower?

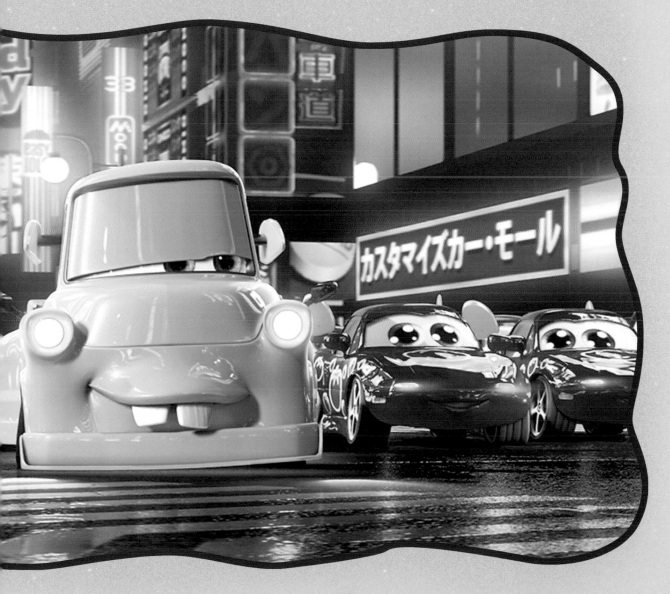

Mater and Kabuto approached the starting line.

The two cars peeled off, leaving a cloud of smoke behind them!

"You can't drift," said Kabuto as the two skidded around a corner. "You are a loser! Ha ha ha!"

"I'll show you!" replied Mater as he poured on the speed—and drove the wrong way down a one-way street!

After a few quick turns, Mater caught up to Kabuto. But the crafty drift racer had a plan.

"Ninjas, attack!" yelled Kabuto. Suddenly, Mater was surrounded!

"Whoa—ninjas? What did you do?" asked Lightning.

"Well, shoot. You oughta know—you was there too!" replied Mater.

Dragon Lightning McQueen arrived just in the nick of time.

"I'll take care of this, dragon style!" said Lightning. One by one, he quickly defeated the ninjas. "Ka-chow!"

Then Mater spotted Kabuto up ahead, almost to the tower.

"Quickly, follow me!" said Lightning.

Lightning and Mater took a shortcut through a construction site. "Whoa! Look at me, I'm drifting!" said Mater as he skidded back and forth. "Wheee-hee!"

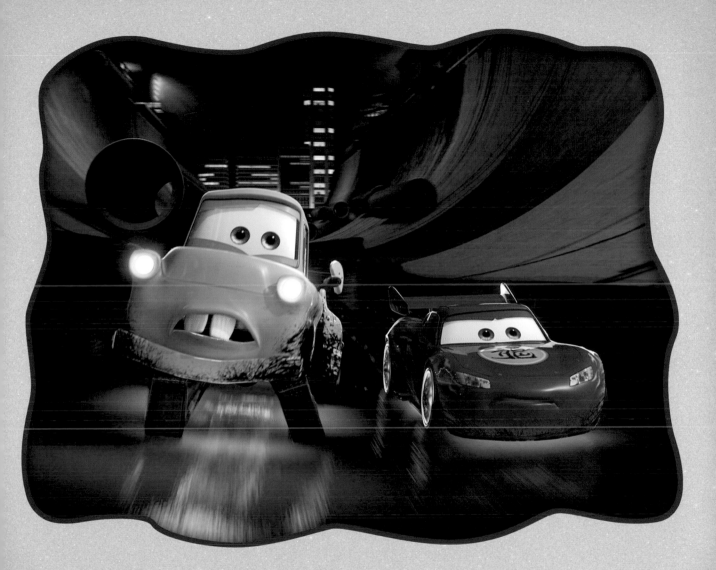

"Oh, no! We're running out of road!" said Mater. "I can't stop!"

"Then GO!" cried Lightning. He gave Mater a shove from behind.

"Cannonball!" screamed Mater as he flew through the air toward Tokyo Tower.

"Victory is mine," Kabuto said to himself—just before Mater landed in front of him. Kabuto was shocked!

"You cannot defeat me!" Kabuto yelled.
"I can too!" said Mater.

"Cannot!" replied Kabuto.

"Can too!" teased Mater.

"Stop saying that!" yelled Kabuto—and he pushed Mater over the rail!

But as he began to fall, Mater lassoed his tow cable to the flagpole on top of Tokyo Tower. He pulled himself up seconds before Kabuto arrived.

"I win," said Mater.

"And that's how I became Tokyo Mater, King of the Drifters," declared Mater proudly.